The Incredible Adventures of

DONOVAN WILLOUGHBY

DEDICATION

To Theresa
for her patience,
love and support

ACKNOWLEDGEMENTS

Special thanks to my buddies
Mark, Dave, Shaunna and Troy.
Also to my parents (Ray and Chris)
for teaching me to dream.

Beautiful America Publishing Company©
Post Office Box 646
Wilsonville, Oregon 97070

Library of Congress Catalog Number 90-42652

ISBN Number 0-89802-551-6

Design: Michael Brugman
Typesetting: Oregon Typesetting
Printed in Hong Kong

The Incredible Adventures of

DONOVAN WILLOUGHBY

Text and Illustrations by
Ray Nelson Jr.

"I don't like it when it rains," sighed Donovan. "You can't play in the park or fly a kite or chase frogs at the pond. All you can do is sit on the front porch and stare."

Donovan and his cat Dexter had been sitting on the porch the entire morning waiting for the skies to clear. It continued to pour and eventually the little boy and his cat fell fast asleep.

A high pitched yelp coming from under the porch suddenly awakened Donovan and Dexter.

"Drats, I know it's here somewhere! Where's that blasted tunnel?" grumbled a muffled voice.

Donovan and Dexter scampered down the steps, crawled through the shrubs and under the porch to investigate the strange noise. "Dexter, what's that moving over in the corner?" asked Donovan.

It took a few minutes for Donovan's eyes to adjust to the darkness.

In the farthest corner a small turtle was poking about. This was not an ordinary turtle. Upon his head he wore a pointy blue hat with stars and moons. Millions of tiny sparks flew from the turtle's fingertips as he searched frantically for the mysterious tunnel. Small bolts of lightning and puffs of blue and orange smoke surrounded the scurrying creature. On the ground, next to the turtle, was a large silver key.

"Who are you?" asked Donovan.

Without stopping his search the turtle replied, "I am Victor Wheezlemott, the Wizard of Alakar. I am searching for the tunnel to take me home. If I don't find the tunnel entrance soon the entire kingdom of Alakar will be forever under the spell of Elmer and Boris Piggy.

"I don't understand," replied a puzzled Donovan.

"It's very simple," said Victor. "The evil Pig Twins, Elmer and Boris, have built an awful machine that will drain Alakar of all its color. They plan to hook this machine up to the end of the Great Alakar Rainbow and pump all of the blues, reds, yellows and greens into their castle. That would leave Alakar a lifeless Kingdom of only black and white."

Victor turned to Donovan and looked at him sadly. "Could you imagine a land with no color? Water that wasn't blue, sunsets with no orange and yellow and grass that wasn't green?"

"At this very moment the pigs are working on the final ingredient that will fuel the wicked machine. Their mission is near completion and I am the only one with the power to stop them from stealing the color for themselves. I only hope I can make it in time."

"Great Goobers! Here it is!" exclaimed Victor. "I've found the tunnel back to Alakar. I must hurry and meet my friend Ursala at the Crayon Forest so that we can stop the Pig Twins."

Without another word the turtle waddled off into the tunnel.

"Wait," yelled Donovan. "We can help you. . .come back!"

It was no use. Victor had scampered off and disappeared into the tunnel.

Donovan and Dexter crawled into the tunnel, but could not find Victor anywhere. They crawled for what seemed like hours when Donovan whispered, "Dex, I think we're lost." The tunnel was dark, damp and musty and Donovan began to cry. "Dexter, we're not going to make it home for dinner."

"Look Donovan, are those lights?" meowed Dexter.

In the distance several small lights were approaching at a rapid pace. Donovan and Dexter could hear singing voices.

"We're the mining earthworms. . .and digging is our thing. We dig throughout the summer, winter, fall and spring."

To Donovan's amazement an empty mining car appeared from behind a small hill. The car screeched to a stop directly in front of the two small adventurers.

Donovan and Dexter inched their way towards the runaway car. Without warning four giant earthworms with large red noses and shiny yellow mining caps popped up sending the two sprawling backward.

"Hey kid. . .what seems to be the problem?" asked the biggest worm.

"Well, Mr. Worm," sniffled Donovan, "it seems we've become quite lost. We were looking for our friend Victor who is heading to Alakar. He was supposed to meet Ursala at the Crayon Forest."

"The Crayon Forest, why didn't you say so. . .we can take you there. Hop in."

Donovan and Dexter climbed into the tiny mining car and settled into their seats.

"How far away is the Crayon Forest?" asked Donovan.

"It's not very far, just over that giant hill and around the bend," answered the worms.

The tiny car trudged slowly. . .clickity clack. . .clickity clack. Up and up, higher and higher they climbed until they reached the peak of the hill. One of the worms turned to Donovan and yelled, "Fasten your seat belts, our brakes don't work very well."

Donovan peeked over the edge of the car to see the steepest hill he had ever seen. The car screamed down the hill. . .faster and faster. Everything became a blur and Donovan could feel his heart pounding. One of the worms grabbed the brake with his tail and pulled. Nothing happened. He pulled again and to his surprise the handle broke. The car was now traveling at an alarming rate and was quickly approaching the bend ahead. Donovan calmly pulled a piece of gum from his pocket and began chewing. Aiming carefully, he tossed the wad of gum onto the track. The car ran over the gum and they screeched to a halt.

"We're here!" exclaimed the worms. "We hope you enjoyed your trip and wish you the best of luck in Alakar."

"Thank you. . .I think. . ." replied Donovan.

Donovan and Dexter turned and waved goodbye as the tiny car chugged off into the darkness.

THE CRAYON FOREST

The buzz of a small neon sign caught the attention of Donovan and Dexter.

"Look Dexter, the sign says we need to climb this ladder to get to Alakar."

Donovan eagerly began climbing. Dexter pushed Donovan up and through the hole. Donovan looked around in amazement. It was the most beautiful thing he had ever seen in his entire life. He had climbed into a valley, but this was like no valley he had ever seen before. Thousands of plants and flowers surrounded a beautiful bluegreen lagoon. There were huge snowcovered mountains around the lagoon reaching all the way to the sky. The most bizarre birds and creatures frolicked about making weird noises. They enjoyed the sunshine filtering down through the giant trees that inhabited the valley.

"Hey, Donovan, pull me up," yelled Dexter.

"Oh yeah, sure Dexter," giggled Donovan. "You're not gonna believe this place."

With Donovan's help, Dexter wriggled through the hole and looked in awe at the incredible valley.

"Dexter, we've got to find that little turtle," said Donovan. "He really needed help in stopping those pigs from stealing the color. I wonder if the Crayon Forest is near by."

"Yes, little man, the Crayon Forest is very near," boomed a voice from above. "And who, may I ask, are you?"

A startled Donovan jumped several feet in the air, landing directly on top of Dexter.

"Who said that?" asked Donovan.

"I did," answered the voice.

It came down from the sky like thunder during a storm. Donovan looked up into the air searching frantically for the source of the rumblings.

"My name is Donovan Willoughby and I am here to help Victor, the wizard, save the Kingdom of Alakar from the Evil Pig Twins."

"That's quite a noble cause for such a little warrior," said the voice from the sky. "Let me introduce myself. My name is Torlock and I am the elder of Crayon Forest."

Donovan hadn't examined the strange trees in the valley very closely. He had noticed the trees were very large and colorful, but now he could see that they were actually giant crayons. It was a forest of colossal crayons. They were hundreds of feet tall. Donovan squinted his eyes and inspected one of the closer trees. At the very top of the nearest crayon he could make out a face.

Suddenly, without warning, the crayon leaned over putting his face down next to Donovan. Donovan didn't run. There was something about the face on the crayon that kept him from trying to escape. A large branch swooped from above and picked up Dexter and Donovan. Up. . .up. . .up. . .the two went until they were eye to eye with the giant crayon. The face on the crayon was a kind and wise face.

"So, young warrior," said Torlock, "you are here to help Victor Wheezlemott in his battle against the Evil Pigs of Alakar. This is a noble cause indeed. If the pigs are successful in stealing all of the color of Alakar they will be the supreme rulers of the kingdom. No one will be able to stop them and many of the creatures in the land will die. If there is anything that we residents of the Crayon Forest can do to help you, just let me know. Within the forest we are quite powerful. Because of our roots, however, we can't travel into other parts of Alakar."

"Would you be so kind as to help me find the magic turtle and Ursala?" asked Donovan.

Torlock replied, "I have not seen Ursala, but if I place you on top of my head you can look across the entire valley."

"That's a great idea," said Donovan. So Torlock lifted Donovan and Dexter and placed them on top of his head. Donovan looked around in amazement. He had never been so high or seen so far. As he looked across the valley he spotted two small figures moving in the direction of Alakar.

"I think I found them!" Donovan shouted. Dexter meowed in agreement.

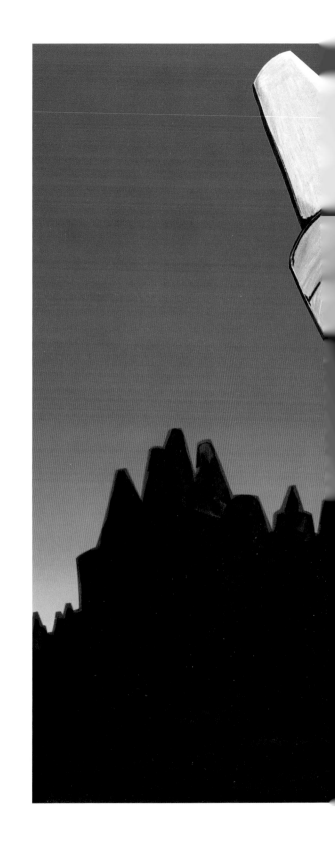

Torlock said, "If you hurry you can catch them before the sun goes down. However, I must warn you, if you stay out after dark the Evil Pig Twins will send their army of mice to search for you."

Donovan said, "Then we must hurry."

Torlock put Donovan and Dexter in his arms, wished them luck, and placed them on the right path to Alakar. "Thank you," said Donovan and he and Dexter ran off to catch Ursala and Victor.

As the sun was setting Donovan and Dexter caught up with Ursala only to find that it was not Victor with her. It was Brandar, her little brother.

"Ursala," Donovan exclaimed, "where is Victor?"

Ursala, with a tear in her eye, sniffled, "He has been captured by the Evil Pig Twins. Brandar and I are going to rescue him."

Donovan knew the only way they could save the kingdom of Alakar was to free Victor so he could use his wisdom and magic to destroy the color machine.

"I have an idea," Donovan said. "Since cats scare mice, and Dexter's a cat, Dexter can protect us from the army of mice."

Dexter looked at Donovan as if to say, "Those mice don't stand a chance with me around." With new found hope, the four friends continued down the path to the Evil Pigs' castle.

As they journeyed closer, the group encountered the swamplands which were nestled at the bottom of the mountain leading to the castle.

"Gee, how are we going to get across the swamp?" asked Donovan.

"Brandar is a real good swimmer so he can take you and Dexter on his back," Ursala replied.

"I don't know if that will work. Dexter doesn't like to get wet. It makes him awful cranky," Donovan said.

Donovan looked at Dexter and Dexter shook his head in agreement and said, "I'm not real heavy, maybe I could sit on top of your head, Ursala. Would you mind?"

"That's alright with me. Just be sure to hold on tight. I'm pretty tall and I'd feel real bad if you fell," said Ursala.

"Not to worry," replied Dexter, "I'll be careful."

The group slowly waded into the swamp water and began to trudge towards the castle.

"Ribbit."

"What was that?" asked Donovan.

"I don't know. It's probably nothing," replied Brandar.

"I said, RIBBIT!"

Wide-eyed, the group looked carefully around the swamp, yet they saw no one.

"I'm over here," exclaimed a large frog sitting on a lilypad. "Are you looking for Victor Wheezlemott?"

"Yes, we are Victor's friends and we're trying to save him," answered Ursala.

"In that case, my name is Omar and I'm here to help you," replied the frog.

"You've seen Victor!!!" exclaimed Donovan.

"Not only have I seen him, but as the Evil Pig Twins were taking him through the swamp, he tossed me something and winked," replied Omar.

"What . . .what was it?" the four said together.

With much anticipation, the excited foursome watched as Omar pulled, from under the lilypad, a large shiny object.

"It's a key," said Omar.

"I recognize that key. It's the magic key Victor was going to use to open the doors of the castle. This will help very much," replied Donovan.

The four thanked Omar for his help and continued on through the swamplands until they reached the bottom of the mountain. The four knew that climbing the mountain would take a long time, and time was running short. They needed to find a fast way to the top of the mountain.

"Hey Dexter," said Donovan, "do you have anymore bubblegum?"

"Yes, but I only have two pieces left," replied Dexter.

"But that means two of us won't be able to get up the mountain," said Donovan.

"That's alright," said Ursala. "I don't think all of the gum in the world would be enough to blow a bubble to lift Brandar and me. We'll climb the mountain and meet you in the castle."

So Donovan and Dexter chewed their bubblegum and blew bubbles until they were lifted off the ground. As they drifted up the side of the mountain they passed over hundreds of mice positioned to protect the castle from intruders. However, in the calm night air, Donovan and Dexter went unnoticed, higher and higher, until they reached the edge of the castle moat.

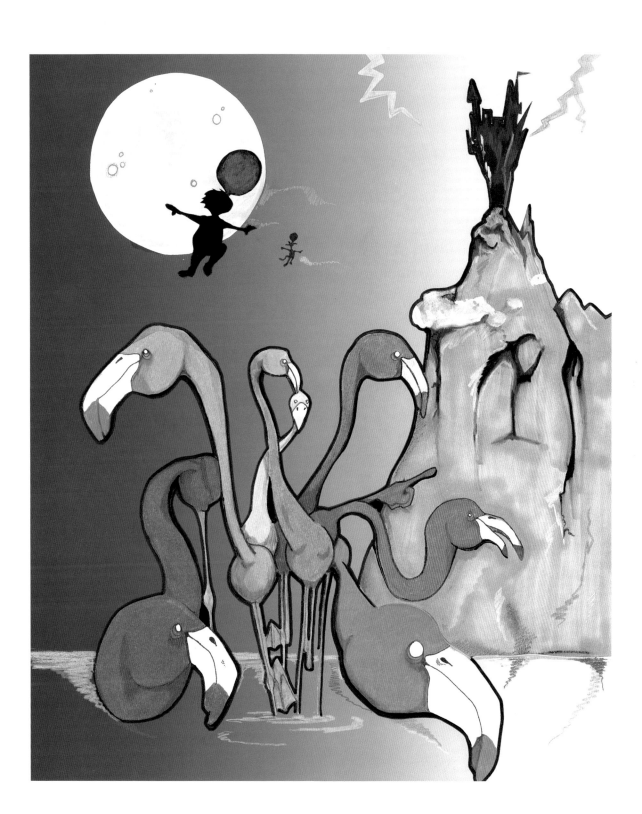

THE CASTLE

At the bank of the castle moat was a large sign.

"What does it say, Donovan?" asked Dexter.

"It says, Beware of Moat Monster."

Crossing the moat would be most dangerous, for within the moat was a ferocious monster who was capable of swallowing them in one gulp. But, in order to save Victor, and the kingdom of Alakar, they knew they must cross the moat and enter the castle.

Dexter, as much as he disliked getting wet, knew that he would have to get in the water to cross the moat. But, he was willing to get his fur wet in order to help his new friends.

As the two of them entered the water, they noticed some ducks swimming towards them.

"Good evening," the ducks cried out.

"Say, you guys haven't seen a giant monster around here have you?" asked Donovan.

"Nope. . .not me. . .I haven't seen anything. . .no one here but us ducks. . .just out for a little swim," replied the ducks.

Unnoticed by Donovan and Dexter, large bubbles began to form on the water just behind the ducks. Suddenly a pair of big pink floppy ears began to surface and a huge monster sprang from the water, startling the ducks. The ducks shot out of the water and flew off into the night, leaving Dexter and Donovan alone with the monster.

"You two weren't trying to get in the castle were you?" asked the monster.

"Uh. . .well. . .uh. . .we were looking for a friend of ours," a frightened Donovan replied.

"Gee, I wish that I had a friend," replied the monster. "Nobody likes me because I'm so big and ugly. You saw the ducks fly off when they saw me."

"Well, I don't think you are ugly," Donovan replied.

"Yeah, you're not ugly," Dexter added. "And, whoever told you that isn't very nice either."

"It was the Pig Twins who told me," said the monster.

"Oh. . .that explains everything," replied Dexter. "By the way, what is your name?"

"My name is Smerlas," he said proudly.

"What do you do out here?" asked Donovan.

"Well, I'm supposed to protect the castle," Smerlas said sadly. "The Pig Twins think I'm mean and evil, but I'm really not."

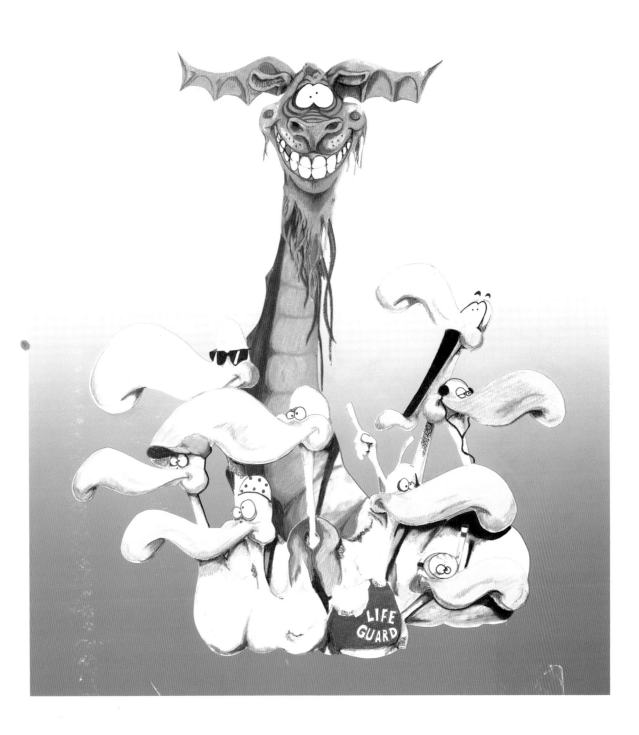

"Do you like the twins . . . are they your friends?" asked Donovan.

"No! They treat me bad and call me names . . . I don't think that's how you treat a friend," said Smerlas.

"I agree! Friends are supposed to be nice to each other. They're not your friends," replied Dexter.

Smerlas realized that Dexter was right. In fact, Dexter and Donovan were the first who had ever stopped and talked to him. Smerlas thought for a moment and decided that Dexter and Donovan were better friends than the Pig Twins had ever been. He listened while Dexter and Donovan explained how the Pig Twins planned to steal the color from the Kingdom of Alakar.

"They can't do that!" exclaimed Smerlas. "I'll help you."

Smerlas picked up Dexter and Donovan in his giant flipper and carried the two toward the castle's drawbridge.

"I'll give you a boost over the drawbridge and then you're on your own. Good luck friends.

THE DUNGEON

Inside the castle the Pig Twins were taking Victor to the Dungeon. They climbed down many, many stairs. The walls became damp and it started to smell bad. At the bottom of these stairs there was a dimly lit room. The Pig Twins tied up Victor and locked him in the room.

"Well, Victor, you will never stop us now," said Boris. "And, once our plan is complete there will be no color in Alakar and we will rule the kingdom forever!!!" The twins laughed evilly and told the guard to watch Victor very carefully.

"Duh, sure boss . . . You can, uh . . . count on me," replied the guard.

Soon, however, the guard became sleepy and began to doze off. Victor realized his chance had come and he began to concentrate. He knew he could use his magic to get the ropes off and even make the guard disappear, but he couldn't unlock the door without the magic key.

"Yummy, yummy tickle my tummy. Binky, inky, sticky and gummy. My aim is true. My purpose is clear. Make these ropes disappear."

POOF!!!

With the ropes gone, Victor crept to the door. The guard, still napping, hadn't heard a thing. Victor pulled his magic wand from his shell and began to chant.

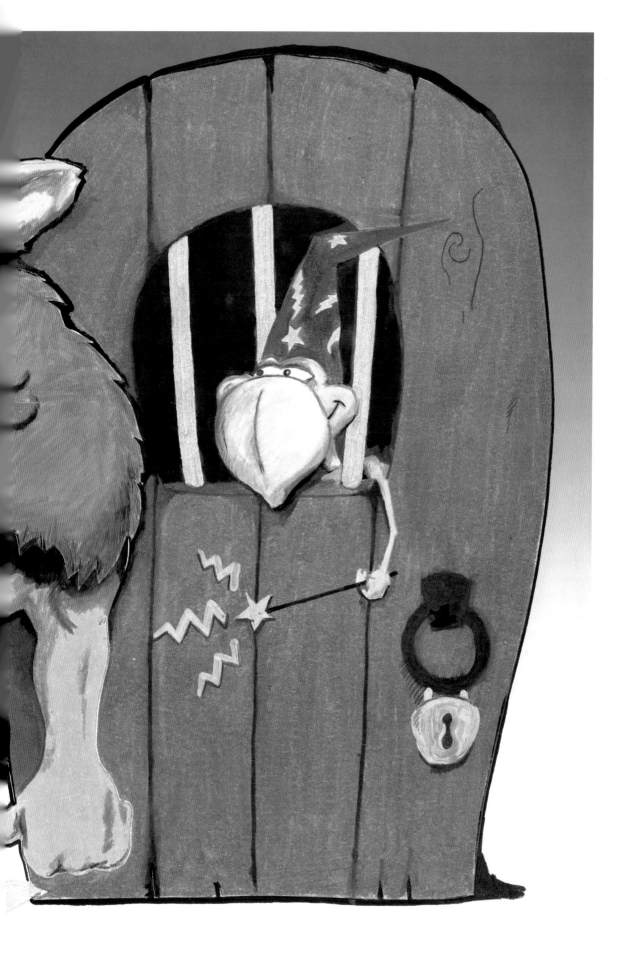

"Apples, bananas. Peaches and pears. Make this guard go upstairs."

POOF!!! The guard was nowhere to be seen.

Victor knew the guard would soon be back and he began to fumble with the lock.

"Drats!" said Victor. "This isn't going to work. . . Purple and green. Blue and orange. . .what rhymes with orange?. . .ugh. . . oh my!"

Just then, Donovan and Dexter scooted past the door. Out of the corner of his eye Donovan noticed a small green head poking out of a door down the hallway.

"Victor, we found you!" exclaimed Donovan. "We've been looking all over and. . ."

"Who are you?" interrupted Victor.

"We're Donovan and Dexter," Donovan said. "We followed you into the tunnel and across Alakar. We want to help you stop the Evil Pig Twins."

"Oh, yes, yes, I remember you," said Victor, "but we can't stop the Twins without the magic key."

"We've got it!" Donovan and Dexter said together.

They unlocked the door and all three bounded up the stairs.

"We haven't much time," Victor said. "We've got to hurry."

THE CUPCAKE

In one of the castle towers, Boris and Elmer were preparing the final element of their plan to rob the kingdom of Alakar of all its color.

"We're almost there, Boris," Elmer said coldly.

A buzzer rang, and Elmer pulled a steaming mound of something from the oven.

"It's done," said Boris. "No one can stop us now!"

As the pigs prepared the finishing touches of their evil plot, Donovan, Dexter and Victor were trying to find their way out of the dungeon. Suddenly, they heard a loud noise behind them.

"Grrrrr!"

"Run!" yelled Victor. "It's the guard."

The guard yelled again and the three adventurers were off. Faster and faster they ran. Turning down this hall and that . . . but they could not lose the guard. As they continued, the halls grew smaller and smaller. Eventually the hallway and doors became so small that the guard could no longer follow the three. Donovan, Dexter and Victor burst through a doorway leaving the guard far behind.

Suddenly, the trio found themselves in bright light and before them stood . . . a very large machine. It was made of all kinds of steel nuts and bolts and pipes, and it seemed to reach the sky.

"This is it!" shouted Victor with glee. "This is the machine we've been looking for. Now . . . if we only knew how to stop it."

Victor, Donovan and Dexter sat next to the machine and began to think. How were they going to stop the Pig Twins?

It was then that Boris and Elmer came into the courtyard. They were carrying an ugly green mound of goo that looked very much like a green cupcake.

"This is it, Elmer," Boris said, "Once we put the spinach cupcake into the machine, we'll be able to rule Alakar forever."

"A spinach cupcake?" whispered Donovan. "I hate spinach!"

"Sshh . . ." said Victor. "We've got to get that cupcake."

Victor, Donovan and Dexter had begun to creep towards the twins when Ursala and Brandar suddenly appeared. They tackled the Pig Twins from behind and the cupcake flew into the air.

"Get it!" yelled Victor.

Donovan jumped forward and caught the cupcake. Suddenly thousands of mice soldiers came out of the castle.

"Now what do we do?" Donovan asked Victor.

"Someone will have to eat the cupcake!" said Victor.

The mice grew closer.

"Yuck!" said Dexter.

"Double yuck!" exclaimed Donovan. "You eat it, Victor."

The mice were very close and the twins began to shout with glee as their army closed in around the trio.

"Quick Donovan, eat the cupcake!" Victor yelled.

Donovan hesitated for a moment, looked towards the mice and then in a few quick bites he ate the cupcake.

"No!!!" screamed Boris and Elmer together.

Suddenly an amazing transformation began to occur. Slowly, Boris, Elmer and the mice turned into black and white statues and the giant machine began to crumble.

"We did it!" cheered Victor, Dexter, Ursala and Brandar. "We've saved the Kingdom of Alakar!"

"Ohhh. . .ughhhh. . .," groaned Donovan. "I ate a spinach cupcake."

"But you saved Alakar," replied Dexter.

Donovan woke up slowly and found himself on his front porch. Dexter woke up as well and the two rubbed their eyes in amazement. They were home. They looked at each other and then looked at the sky. It had stopped raining and there before them was the most beautiful rainbow they had ever seen. The colors were bright and alive, they seemed to glow.

"We did it, Dexter," Donovan said. "We saved the Kingdom of Alakar. And, we even made it back in time for dinner."

"Mom! Mom!" yelled Donovan as he and Dexter ran into the house. "What's for dinner? What smells so good?"

"It's a new cupcake recipe I found—I think you'll like it!"